I0718164

little moments we lost

Zack Beer

little moments we lost

Radical Bookshop and Press
4838 Richard Road SW, Suite 300
Calgary, AB T3E 6L1

Copyright 2021 by Radical Bookshop and Press

FIC029000 - Fiction, Short Stories

All rights reserved. No part of this publication may be reproduced, stored in a retrieval system or transmited in any form or by any means, electronic, mechanical, photocopying, recording or otherwise without the prior permision of the author.

Chinook Blast Collection
Volume 1
February 1, 2021

Editors: Lexie Angelo
Cover Design: Lexie Angelo

ISBN-13: 978-1-990201-10-3

Printed in the United States

Typeset in Caslon Pro

To every queer person who has experienced and lost little moments.

contents

Acknowledgements

About the Author

Special Thanks

A smirk

The clock ticked 8:30 and I let out a sigh. Throughout the lecture hall, three other people spread out, each of us wondering how late the prof would be today. We sat in a windowless room, in a forgotten annex of the building, a fine place to succumb to the weight of a non-descript October morning. I typed *Twitter* into the search bar on my laptop and streamed through threads and threads of cottagecore aesthetic photos, political rants, and Aries daily horoscopes. I startled upright when a pile of books crashed onto the desk next to me, almost toppling my travel mug.

"This seat taken?" You asked.

"Have you seen anyone sit here for the last four weeks?" I replied.

"Great," you said sitting down.

Silence stretched out between us as people shuffled into the room. I refused to look away from my computer until I glanced at you doodling in your notebook, and the hair on the back of my neck stood alert. The professor dawdled in, only thirty-five minutes late (a new personal best for him). He droned on about 19th-century imperialism, not sensing that nobody in the soul-sucking room could give a fuck.

Grey carpets on grey walls on grey desks on grey people. You spoiled my melodrama and slid your notebook onto my desk. *He sucks ass.* Our eyes locked for a moment, and a smirk stretched across your face.

A blush

The hallway bustled like a colony of ants. Students sauntered along with their friends, sat curled up on the couches, rocked out to music blaring through headphones, canvassed for equality between animals and humans, and rushed for their classes. We sat leg-to-leg on a butt-worn two-person seat against the wall of the hallway, watching the students pass us by.

"I hate him," I said. "He seriously tried to teach us that colonialism in India was a good thing. And he wants us to cite like we're dinosaurs. He hasn't stepped foot into a history class since the '80s when he got his Ph.D."

A moment passed and a chuckle bubbled from deep in your chest.

"No, you're right, this class is awful," you replied.

"What's funny?" I asked.

"When I woke up this morning, I didn't imagine I'd be accosted by a cute nerd from class."

My face scorched. Red blood cells vibrated in my chest, shooting through my body. I sucked in a breath, memorizing the sharply sweet scent of your peppermint cologne; elbowing your arm, laughter emanated from our couch and washed away in the flood of people.

A kiss

Fog ambled through the tree-lined street framed by lithe incandescence. The sounds of the distant freeway echoed through fog, insulating the bumble of cars and the rumble of pavement.

"This is my street, I can walk from here," I said. You chuckled, reached for my hand and tugged me down the road. Stumbling through the fog, your arm snaked along the small of my back, holding me closer to you as we walked. Each vein in my body palpitated against my skin as I followed suit with my arm along your back until I slipped my palm into your back pocket. Our pace continued and I peeked at the smirk cracked across your face. "This is it," I said, stopping in front of the gate.

"I guess this is goodnight."

"Guess so." The blush returned as you cupped my face and pulled me in. Our lips touched only for a moment, and you pulled away.

"I've never kissed a man before," you said, your hand still cupping the back my neck.

"Me either."

A toast

Cheesy Italian music floated through the room as the flavours of garlic and cheap parmesan cheese coated my tongue. I took a sip of water, but it did not help with the hunger-induced cottonmouth. The restaurant around us buzzed as servers in jeans and T-shirts fluttered around the room, filling glasses with tepid tap water and boxed wine that tasted all the more ethereal. Standing up in my seat, I reached across the table and adjusted your shirt collar for the third time.

"I cannot imagine the neck gymnastics you must do to constantly mess up your clothes," I said. You took my hand in yours and held it atop the table.

"This is seriously where you wanted to come?"

"Hey, they have the best five-dollar drinks on this side of the Bow."

"Can't argue with that."

Your eyes lit up with giddy excitement as the waiter came over and placed your carbonara with extra green onions and my spicy sausage penne. The server poured chardonnay into our glasses as I vibrated, eyes locked firmly onto my plate of carb-filled goodness.

"Wait—" he said.

I paused holding a forkful of pasta.

"To our one year," he said holding up his glass.

 I grabbed my wine and we clinked our bargain beverages together.

A proposal

"Would you marry me?" you asked. Dark brown eyes bore into mine as you laid back against the couch, unflinching. I muted the television. Green and blue lights from the nature documentary danced across your face and the whir of the refrigerator hummed from under the silent apartment.

"My answer hasn't changed since the last time you asked me," I replied. Your jaw grumbled as you bit down and ground your teeth.

"Why?" Those deep eyes betrayed no emotion. Steady. Rigid. Brittle.

"What do you want from me?" I asked, pulling my feet up on the loveseat and turning so we were face-to-face. My cat jumped up onto the back of the sofa just beside my head, stark white against the cracked black pleather.

"Anything other than no," you said. Your eyes flickered from mine. Reaching down to grab a hold of my hand, your thumb grazed along my knuckles.

"If I thought it would make both of us happy, I would've said yes," I said, staring into those eyes. A moment passed.

"I'm not ready yet. I will be — and I'll tell you when I am."

I once again faced the television and used my freehand to unmute the volume. You pulled our hands, still entangled, into your lap and turned attention to the movie.

"I am in love with you."

"And I *am* in love with you," I replied, laying my head onto your shoulder, hearing your heartbeat throughout your body.

"Will you move in with me?" He asked.

"That, I will definitely do."

A bird

"The store didn't have any of the tools you wanted, so I just got a screwdriver," I said kicking the door closed behind me. Brown carboard boxes framed the entryway and lined a clear path into the house. "I also stopped at the weed store because apparently moving makes me want to rip my eyes out." I pulled the jacket from my shoulders and threw it down next to the unassembled coat rack. "Hello?" I called into the house. You rounded the corner, shirt soaked in splotchy blood.

"I caught a bird," you said.

"You caught a *what*?"

"A pigeon," you said, disappearing behind the corner. "Come on, she's in here," you called from the bedroom. Dropping the bag to the floor, I ran after you.

"How did a bird get in here?" I shouted.

"I was making a tuna melt, but then it started to get a little smoky, so I opened the back door," you said. I rounded the corner into the bedroom, and saw you standing over a bundle of blankets on the floor; your knees slightly bent, hand out in front of you, fear flashing in your eyes. "I left the room to get another box. I guess a bird flew in and started to wreak havoc."

"Why are you covered in blood?" I asked.

"Vanessa attacked it while I tried to get the bird out."

"You let my cat attack a disgusting sky-rat?"

"Vanessa will be fine, I locked her in the other room," you said, lowering your voice as you crept closer to the bundle of blankets. "I think this bird is terrified. I tried to get it into a bucket but, well —"

You placed your hands on the blanket. The mound of fabric and bird bulged out at the touch as she shifted, and you jumped back, barely containing a yelp.

"Go get me some oven mitts," I said. You nodded in agreement and left to grab some. The blanket fluttered at the bird's movements, spasmic, and covered in the cartoon owls adorning the fabric. You came back into the room and handed me the kitchen gloves. Putting them on, I crept towards the trapped pigeon. Birds can smell fear, and it was definitely more afraid of me than I was of it, but maybe not more than you were. I crept down to the bundle and slowly folded the edge of the blanket, hands meeting underneath, keeping the bird solidly inside the blanket. "I'm going to set her on the balcony, get the door."

Step after step towards the door, movements steady, calm, I set her in the middle of the wooden deck. I retreated slightly and pulled the fabric from the bird. She burst out, claws, wings, and beak snapping and flapping. A talon sliced a jaggedly thin line across the back of my palm, she turned around, and flapped her wings away. I stumbled back into you, only to feel your arms wrap around me.

"Are you okay?" You mumbled into my ear. I turned around and placed a kiss onto your lips for just a moment and pulled away.

"Peachy," I said. Reaching out to tug at his shirt, I said, "Go change your shirt. I'll check to make sure my cat is okay. Then you are taking me to the doctor."

"I thought you were 'peachy'?"

"We have no idea what kind of deplorable diseases that pigeon carried. I don't want to start our first day living together with rabies."

"Birds can't have rabies," you said, "but you'd look adorable in a hospital gown."

"Still," I replied, standing on the ball of my feet to kiss his cheek once more.

A silence

Tiny windswept waves lapped against the shore. Your eyes gazed at the mountain behind the lake as rocky pebbles dug into my ass beneath the blanket. My hands folded through yours, both of us staring forward as our breath misted in the air. You were supposed to leave that night. Only for six months. Only to take care of your mother during her treatment. Only, I couldn't leave. I made the choice to stay and you made the choice to go. Moments screamed in my head.

"We can push it back," you said.

"I know."

"I'll miss you."

"I know."

But we spoke into the unchangeable void. I pulled you closer to me. I wanted to feel your heart beating through your jacket, but everything between us was muffled. We watched the little waves and the tottering, trembling trees until we had to go.

A scream

My eyes convulsed open. A high-pitched tone rang continuously in my ear, just out of reach. Blood rushed down my face, dripping onto my shirt. Your hand lay in mine. The deflated airbag descended onto my lap, covered in shards of glass twinkling like mountain snow. Frigid fog and winter air rushed into the car through the jagged edges of the windshield. Bones crunched in my leg as I shifted in the seat. The ring jumped an octave in my head. I pulled myself upwards, my entire body wailing at movement, leg stuck. I sucked in a deep breath and looked down. Underneath the steering wheel, the car crunched inward, holding my calf in place. White bone soaked in red peeked at me from just below the metal. The ringing hit a crescendo, then silence.

And then overwhelming noise. Sirens screeched, people cried, paramedics yelled at firefighters and firefighters yelled back. A man retched in the distance, vomit splattering onto the pavement like a dropped egg. My hand tightened around yours; but yours didn't squeeze back. Gasped breaths wracked my lungs, each one quicker than the last as I turned my body to see yours. I reefed my leg from underneath the metal. Blood flowed from the wound as pops and cracks were framed by people's screams. You lay in the passenger seat. Over your face, red and blue lights scintillated your features. Your eyes stayed closed as I shook your body, chest neither rising nor falling. I screamed. For help. For you. For anything.

A sob

The hallway bustled like a colony of ants. People sauntered with their friends – ignored their pain, confronted their demons, hid from each other behind simple, happy facades, and ran for their classes they could not fail because it was their last chance; people far too busy to notice me stumbling through them. I pulled the mickey of swishing vodka from my pants pocket, which apparently was offensive enough to warrant attention. Good, maybe if they witnessed my supposed pain, I could actually feel it for myself. Who cared about a drunk on a university campus anyways? Ignoring the shooting looks of derision, I pushed through a door to find the grey room. Grey carpets on grey walls on grey desks, but no grey people; just me, alone in a dark windowless room. I plunged into the chasm, back against the wall. I heaved sobs until someone found me and called campus security.

A call

"I miss Alex," she said, as her voice frizzled over the phone. She still refused to upgrade to a cell phone.

"I know," I replied as my hands shook. I felt a dull ache in my legs and jumped up from my chair. "I didn't think today would be so hard."

A moment passed through the phone. Her choked sobs crackled in my ear as tears streaked down my face.

"I still bought a cake," she said. "Every year, I bought him one even when he couldn't eat it from across the country."

I paced without speaking as more tears flowed.

"Now I get to fucking sit here with a cake for my dead son."

She took a deep breath. Then another. I watched the clock strike 8:30 a.m.

"I have to go. I'm going to be late for my final and you have your last chemo treatment today," I said. "It's a big day for both of us. But I'll call again tonight." She sucked in a breath and wished me luck. I reciprocated. We hung up.

Rounding the corner of our kitchen to retrieve my bag, I grabbed a thermos from the sink and opened up the freezer; it was the best place to keep the vodka. The bottle glugged until the thermos filled halfway, the remaining space filled with day old coffee from the counter. I replaced the alcohol in its home and closed the door. Staring at me, held onto the fridge with one of your dog magnets was a card:

You are invited to the wedding of

Alex Henderson and Jacob Wallock

Save the date.

The door locked firmly behind me as I fled the house, catching the bus to the university, determined to make the call that night.

ACKNOWLEDGEMENTS

There are several people I would like to acknowledge. Primarily, my parents, Crista and Anthony, along with my siblings Josh, Caleb and Kassidy. I would also like to recognize my friends Bret Crowle, Alex Whittaker O'Rourke, and Mark Johnson, who helped me edit and comb through draft after draft of this story, offering their support and encouragement throughout the entire process. Lastly, I would like to thank my writing teachers, Micheline Maylor and Karen Overbye, who taught me everything I know about writing.

ABOUT THE AUTHOR

Zack Beer is an emerging writer and museum professional currently living in Calgary, Alberta. They attend Mount Royal University, where they study history and creative writing. They have a fascination with gender and sexuality throughout history and in literature.

Zack can be found on:

Twitter @zack_beer

Instagram @zachary_beer

And his website: www.zackbeer.com

SPECIAL THANKS

Chinook Blast Festival

The City of Calgary

Tourism Calgary

Calgary Municipal Land Corporation

Calgary Arts Development

Calgary Public Library

IngramSpark

www.ingramcontent.com/pod-product-compliance
Lightning Source LLC
Chambersburg PA
CBHW032025180726

48283CB00008B/2818